DRAGON GAMES

DRAGON GAMES

THE BATTLE FOR IMPERIA

BY MADDY MARA

SCHOLASTIC INC.

ISBN 978-1-338-85196-0

10 9 8 7 6 5 4 3 2 1 23 24 25 26 27

Printed in the U.S.A. 40

First printing 2023

Book design by Stephanie Yang

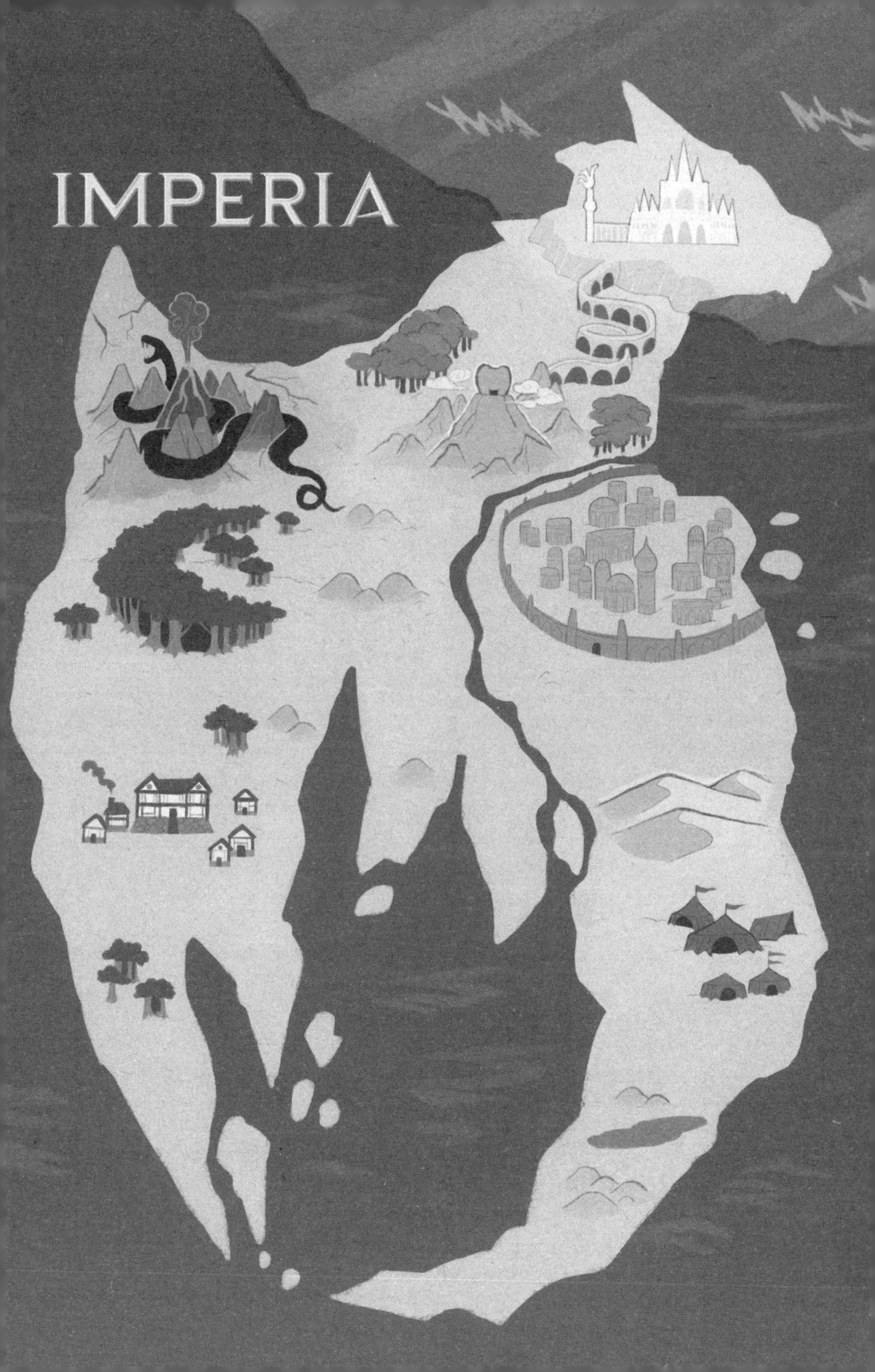

IMPERIA

Luca hurried into the school cafeteria. Lunchtime was nearly over, but he had to eat something! As he was grabbing a tray, the doors swung open. A girl with dark hair and green eyes rushed in.

"Yazmine!" Luca was surprised. Yazmine was not the type of person who ran late for anything.

"I've been trying to make it here all

lunchtime," Yazmine said, also taking a tray. "Ms. Long asked me to return some books to the library."

"She got me to take our camp forms to the principal. I just got here, too," Luca said.

He felt a little awkward. He and Yazmine didn't really talk much at school. They had totally different friend groups. But they had been on a couple of big adventures together in a mysterious land called Imperia. They were part of a three-person team trying to bring dragons back to Imperia.

Luca had seen Yazmine in dragon form. She'd seen him in dragon and beast form. But they'd never eaten lunch together.

"What would you like?" asked a bored-looking woman behind the counter.

There wasn't much food left. Luca and Yazmine looked at the gloopy pumpkin soup and shriveled fries.

"I guess I'll take the soup, please," Luca said.

"Fries for me, thanks," Yazmine said.

As the server began dishing out their food, the cafeteria doors opened again. Someone hurried in, running his fingers through his hair. It was Zane: football star and third member of the Imperia team.

"Any food left?" he asked. "I'm starving!"

The woman serving smiled at him. She didn't look bored anymore. "You're Zane, right?"

This woman was new at the school cafeteria. How did she already know Zane's name?

But Zane didn't seem surprised. He was used to everyone knowing who he was. "Yup," Zane said cheerily.

The server reached below the counter. When she straightened up, she was holding a steaming bowl of spaghetti and meatballs.

"For you," she said, handing the bowl to Zane.

"Wait, what?" Yazmine said, outraged. "How come he gets that and we get sorry leftovers?"

"Special order." The woman shrugged. "You'd better eat quickly. Bell's going to ring in ten minutes."

Luca, Yazmine, and Zane sat at the nearest

table. A strained silence fell. The three of them never sat together at school.

Yazmine speared a soggy fry with her fork and nibbled the end. Luca looked at his soup. Maybe it tasted better than it looked? He tried it. Nope. Worse. Definitely worse.

Only Zane was enjoying his food.

Luca frowned. Why had Zane gotten a special meal?

Luca looked up as Ms. Long, their teacher, stuck her head around the half-opened door. "Ah, there you three are. I am glad you're eating. You're going to need a lot of energy this afternoon."

"Why?" Yazmine asked eagerly.

Clearly, she was thinking the same thing as Luca: Were they returning to Imperia?

Ms. Long just smiled. “I’ll see the three of you later.”

Then the door closed again.

“This is SO good!” Zane said, shoveling in mouthfuls of spaghetti.

Yazmine eyed it enviously. “That’s a huge serving. There’s no way you’ll eat all that. How about you share?”

“Of course I’ll eat it all.” Zane looked insulted. “But sure, you can share.”

“Thanks!” said Yazmine and Luca at the same time.

Zane was annoying sometimes, but he could also be generous.

Luca stuck his spoon into the spaghetti and tried to twirl the strands around it. As he lifted it, the pasta slipped off. He really needed a fork. He tried again, this time digging the spoon in deeper. His utensil hit something.

"There's something hard in there," Luca said.

"What do you mean?" Zane stuck his fork deep into the mountain of pasta. There was a muffled *clink* as Zane's fork made contact with . . . something.

The three teammates looked at one another.

Luca's pulse sped up. Something was about to happen. He could feel it.

Yazmine attacked the pasta, sending meat-balls flying. One of them flicked out of the bowl, pinging Zane on the nose.

"Hey, careful!" he said, wiping off the sauce and then licking his finger.

Yazmine paid him no attention. "Look!"

There, at the bottom of the huge bowl, was a rock, draped with strands of spaghetti.

Luca leaned forward. "Is that a Thunder Egg?" he asked doubtfully.

The last two Thunder Eggs they'd returned to Imperia had been football-sized. This thing was no bigger than a baseball.

"Come on, Luca! What else would it be?" Yazmine teased. "A giant meatball?"

"Maybe!" Zane grinned. "Let me check." Zane reached into the bowl. The moment his fingers took hold of the strange lump, the room plunged into darkness.

2

Excitement and nerves gripped Luca as he somersaulted through the inky blackness.

This was their third trip into Imperia. Where would they land this time? Would it be someplace new? It was also their third time competing against the power-hungry Dartsmith. This round would be the most important and dangerous of all.

Only when the three dragons return will Imperia have peace again.

Luca, Yazmine, and Zane had already returned two Thunder Eggs to the land. Inside these eggs were the future dragon rulers of Imperia. And now they had the third one. If Luca and his teammates managed to safely return this Thunder Egg to its rightful home, the ancient prophecy would be fulfilled.

And if they failed? Well, Luca didn't want to even think about that!

Luca felt the ground beneath him. The darkness faded, and Luca blinked as he looked around. He was near a stone wall—sturdy, ancient, and very high. Was it part of a building?

Luca stood up, brushing off the dirt and grass. He was no longer wearing his normal track pants. Instead he was wearing strange leather pants and heavy boots. At his feet was the Thunder Egg. It still had a single strand of spaghetti on it. Quickly, Luca removed the pasta and stowed the egg safely in the bag he found slung across his shoulders.

He was glad to be in charge of looking after it. During the last trip, Zane had been in charge of the Thunder Egg, and he had not been nearly careful enough.

"So you're the human this time!" said a voice.

It sounded like Zane but way louder. Luca had already guessed that Zane would be a dragon this time, but somehow it was still a surprise to see the transformation. Zane was a massive dragon, for one thing. Far bigger than Luca or Yazmine had been. His scales were a shiny gray, almost metallic. This made him look like he was wearing armor.

Zane stretched out his steely wings and roared, flames erupting from his mouth. "I had to wait until last to be a dragon. But I always knew I'd be the best one."

"Let's wait and see about that," came Yazmine's voice.

Luca looked around. Where was Yazmine, exactly? From the shadows, a black shape emerged. It was a huge, puma-like beast with bright green eyes. Muscles rippled beneath its sleek fur as the beast stalked toward Luca, tail swishing.

"Yaz?" Luca asked nervously. There were a lot of strange creatures in Imperia, and not all of them were friendly. If this beast wasn't Yazmine, things could go horribly wrong very quickly.

"What's up, Luca?" growled the beast, flashing its sharp white teeth. "Worried I'm going to bite?"

Before he could respond, the beast leapt through the air and landed at Luca's feet. Startled, Luca stepped back and knocked against the stone wall . . . and promptly fell right through it!

Dazed, he scrambled to his feet and looked

around. *He was on the other side of the wall!* Before him stretched a narrow street, lined with old buildings. The windows were without glass and a large tree was growing out of one of the roofs. Tangled vines dripped from its branches.

It was the strangest-looking tree Luca had ever seen.

But, then, this whole place was strange to him. It was wrapped in a thick silence. Everything seemed long deserted. There was something very creepy about it.

"Luca, where are you?" Yazmine called. "Sorry! I didn't mean to scare you."

"I'm on the other side of the wall!" Luca yelled back. He reached out to touch the stone wall, and his hand went right through. He gave the others a wave. "Guess walking through solid stuff is my special power."

"What can you see in there?" Zane asked in his booming dragon voice.

"I'm in some kind of city," Luca replied. "But it's totally deserted. I'll just take a quick look before I come back."

Luca crossed the potholed street to the building with the tree growing through its roof. It was a peculiar-looking place. The front door was large, and the windows seemed impossibly high. No human would be able to see out of them. The outer wall was crumbling, and caked with dust and dirt.

Luca brushed away the dirt to reveal painted scenes of dragons. Near the door was a statue of a dragon. Its jaws were open, as if roaring a greeting. Or a warning.

Luca felt a rush of excitement. "I think dragons used to live here!" he called to his friends. He tried to imagine how this place might have looked back when the city was filled with those incredible creatures.

The Thunder Egg in Luca's bag seemed warmer now, like it was heated by the memory of those fiery beasts.

There was a sudden noise. It was a creaky sort of whisper. Luca's heart thumped. *What was that?*

"Luca? You'd better come back." Yazmine's growly beast voice had a hint of worry in it. "I sense something's not right about this place."

Luca could feel it, too. He headed back across the road, hoping it would be as easy to get through the wall a second time. Halfway across, Luca tripped in one of the giant potholes. As he righted himself, Luca heard a rustling, whooshing sound from above.

It's just Zane, he told himself. *He's probably flown over the wall to have a look.*

But the sound was coming from the tree growing through the roof. The branches spread wide to reveal a green face on the trunk. Curling vines dripped from its mouth like tongues. Its beady red eyes were fixed on Luca. Luca froze as the nasty face leaned forward and breathed in deeply.

Was it . . . *smelling* him? A sharp-toothed smile stretched across its cracked face.

"Luca!" shouted Yazmine from the other side. She sounded really worried now. "Get out of there!"

As she spoke, the tree monster thingy bent

toward Luca. Old roof tiles flew in all directions as it pulled its roots free. With its red eyes still fixed on Luca, the monster leapt into the air.

3

Finally, Luca unfroze. Turning his back on the monster, he ran toward the high wall. His thoughts raced. He had no idea how his moving-through-walls power worked. Like, did it work every time? Did he have to do it in a particular way? He had stuck his hand through the wall before. But maybe that was just luck.

He heard a thud as the monster hit the

ground. Luca was only a few steps from the wall now. He was going to make it! But, inches from the wall, Luca went sprawling. The bag containing the egg slammed into the rock-strewn road.

Thwack!

Luca winced. Had he just broken the *third and final Thunder Egg*?

There was no time to check. As he tried to get to his feet, Luca felt something holding him. The monster had wrapped a vine around his ankle! And now the vine was rapidly winding up his leg. Luca pulled at the vine, quickly unwinding it. He jumped to his feet, but another vine had now taken hold of his wrist. Even worse, a third flung out and latched on to his face. The tendrils wrapped around his mouth so he couldn't call out.

Luca kicked at the plant-monster, sending tendrils and leaves flying. But the creature grabbed his flailing leg again. Luca felt panic building as the monster started to squeeze. How on earth was he going to free himself?

"What's going on?" Zane called. "It sounds like you're wrestling a tree over there."

A shadow fell across Luca as he struggled to get the vine off his face. Zane was hovering above him.

"Oh!" Zane said. "You *are* wrestling a tree. That's a Fear Stalker by the looks of it. I was kinda hoping we'd meet one. Ms. Long said they track you by sniffing out your fear.

Pretty wild, huh? It's even more terrifying than I imagined."

Luca waved his one free arm at Zane. Now was not the time to be admiring the local monsters!

Luckily, Zane seemed to get it. He took a deep breath and roared. Bright flames surged out, singeing the monster's leaves and branches. A bonfire smell filled the air. With a furious shriek, the Fear Stalker let go of Luca's arm and mouth. But the monster grabbed his flailing leg again.

Luca flung himself forward. He could just reach far enough to push one hand through the wall. He felt around for something to grab hold of. Maybe he could pull himself free.

Above him, Zane roared again, and Luca felt the heat sear his skin. "Go easy on the flames!" he called.

"Do you want me to free you or not?" grumbled the huge dragon.

"I appreciate your help. But I'd rather not

end up a lump of charcoal in the process!" Luca yelled back.

Luca's hand on the other side of the wall made contact with something furry.

"That's my back leg," called Yaz in her beast voice. "Grab on. I'm going to pull you through."

Luca wrapped his fingers around Yaz's strong, furry leg. Would this work? What if the Fear Stalker didn't let go? Would he end up pulling in Yazmine?

Stay calm! Luca reminded himself.

Now that Zane had identified the monster, Luca could recall things about it. Ms. Long had said that the best way to deal with a Fear Stalker was to keep your fear under control.

Fear Stalkers smell the slightest sweat. They can even sense if your heart is racing.

Luca breathed out slowly, trying to calm his pulse. He gripped hard onto Yaz's leg.

"On the count of three!" she growled. "One . . . two . . ."

On *three* Yazmine surged forward, pulling Luca with her. At the same time, Zane roared once more. The Fear Stalker creaked again and finally loosened its grip on Luca. Quickly, Luca tucked his legs up and away from the vines. He was halfway through the wall now, his head on one side and his legs on the other. He really hoped he wouldn't get stuck there!

Yaz lunged again, and a moment later, Luca tumbled onto the grass outside the wall.

"Are you okay?" asked Yaz, leaping over to him.

"I think so," said Luca, standing up. He tested out his ankle. It was sore but not broken. Then he remembered the egg hitting the ground. With a trembling hand, Luca opened the bag and pulled it out.

To his relief, the egg was still in one piece. But as he looked closer, his heart plunged. Right at the tip of the precious object was a fine crack!

"What happened?" Zane asked, landing beside Luca.

"I tripped and the egg hit the ground," Luca blurted out.

"Hey, I almost handed the egg to Dartsmith

last time we were here," Zane said. "It happens, right?"

Luca felt even worse now. He'd been so hard on Zane for being careless when he was in charge of the egg.

"What happens if it breaks before we can fulfill the prophecy?" Luca wondered out loud.

"It's only a small crack," said Yazmine. "Let's just hope it doesn't get any bigger. We need to get away from here. I have a feeling the Fear Stalker hasn't given up on us yet!"

Even as she spoke, there was loud rustling and a *thump*. The Fear Stalker appeared at the top of the stone wall. Had it climbed up there or jumped? Either option was equally bad!

Zane spread his wings. "Jump on my back," he instructed Luca. "Yazmine, I guess you can run fast enough to get away from that overgrown houseplant?"

"Probably. But I think I'll fly," Yazmine said coolly, untucking two wings.

"You've got wings?" Luca said in disbelief as he leapt onto Zane's back. "Zane and I could only run in beast form!"

"I got lucky, I guess," said Yazmine, flapping her wings and rising into the air. "But right now that's just a teensy bit less important than getting away from this monster!"

4

Luca held tight as Zane took off into the air. The Fear Stalker flung its vines like lassos, trying to grab hold of them as they escaped. But they were soon well out of reach, zooming up toward the clouds.

"That was intense," Yazmine said, flying alongside Zane and Luca. "Luca, check the Thunder Egg. I want to see if we earned any points."

The egg! Luca's heart skipped a beat. What if he'd ruined their chances of fulfilling the prophecy? All three eggs had to be brought home before dragons could return to Imperia.

Luca hated to think that he might have messed up everything.

He opened the bag and carefully extracted the Thunder Egg. The score glowed.

–1:0

Luca held out the egg so Yazmine could see.

"What?" growled Yazmine. "We've LOST a point!"

"That can't be right," Zane said, turning as he flew so he could see it. "We just escaped from a daisy with anger-management issues. Why would our score go down?"

"It's probably because of the crack." Luca sighed. "I think it's gotten bigger."

"Oh yeah," said Zane. "That'd be it."

Yazmine didn't say anything. Luca guessed she was trying not to bite his head off. Damaging the egg was bad enough. Causing them to lose points made it even worse.

Luca looked back at the egg. "The map's appeared!"

Below the zigzagging crack, the familiar outline of Imperia was glowing. A tooth-shaped symbol flashed.

"Looks like we need to head for Wisdom Mountain," said Luca, showing Zane which direction to fly. "The Ancient Ones must have something to tell us."

From the corner of his eye Luca spotted something heading their way. He stiffened. Was it Dartsmith's drones? But no, it was a flock of small, multicolored birds. They seemed to be in a tremendous hurry and kept crashing into one another. Each time they did, they squeaked loudly and changed color.

"Watch where you're going!" Zane roared as the flock flew dangerously close.

The birds chirped excitedly. On their last visit to Imperia, Luca had been in beast form so he could understand the animals. But this time, in human form, Luca couldn't understand the birds at all.

He looked over at Yazmine, who was still flying alongside. "Can you understand them?"

Yazmine's green eyes were wide. "I can!" she purred. "But it's hard to make it out. It's something about the big day finally coming. And a big battle, I think? I have no idea what any of it means."

With loud squawking, the birds swooped high in a showy formation.

Zane snorted, sending smoke streaming into the air. "Those birds think they're better at flying than me? Well, I'll show them!"

"Don't, Zane!" Luca yelled, clutching the bag with the Thunder Egg. "Just ignore them. We've got to get to the Dragon Cave."

But Zane wouldn't listen. He flapped his powerful, steely wings and surged upward, flying directly into the flock.

The birds scattered in all directions, changing colors like a flying disco ball.

Zane laughed a deep, dragon-y laugh. "Being a dragon is the BEST!" he declared. "I can't believe you guys didn't try out more stunts when you were dragons."

“There’s this thing called ‘focus,’ ” Yazmine retorted. “You might like to give it a try. Like, now.”

But again, Zane wasn’t listening. “Hold on tight, Luca!” he called.

Luca only just had time to fling his arms around Zane’s scaly neck before the dragon began to spin around and around midair.

“Zane! STOP!” Luca yelled. Not only was he worried about the Thunder Egg, but the spinning was making him sick.

“Oh, come on!” Zane called back. “This is fun! There’s no need to worry. I could fly with my eyes closed. Hey, that’s an idea. Let’s try it.”

"Zane, don't!" Yazmine growled, sounding stern.

By the wild way Zane was flying, it was clear Zane was doing it anyway. Rather than flying in a straight line, he began whooshing up and down, like he was riding a roller coaster.

Luca screwed his own eyes shut and clung on. *I will not throw up. I will not throw up*, he chanted to himself.

"WATCH OUT!" Yazmine shrieked.

Luca opened his eyes in time to see that they were flying dangerously low—and heading directly for a massive boulder! There was no way Zane was going to be able to swerve in time.

Protecting the Thunder Egg with his body, Luca leaned forward and wrapped one arm around Zane's neck. He reached up to put the other hand on Zane's head. Luca wasn't sure why he did it. He just felt like he needed to.

He braced himself for impact . . . but it never came.

A moment later, Zane was skidding to a stop on a patch of grass. Luca turned around. The giant boulder was behind them! Luca checked his bag. The Thunder Egg was still in one piece.

Yazmine landed beside them. "That was incredible!"

"My awesome flying skills?" Zane grinned. "Why thank you, Yaz."

Yazmine rolled her eyes. "The flying was reckless. But the way you both went straight through that rock was amazing. Luca, how did you get Zane to go through with you?"

"I'm not sure," Luca admitted. "But I put one hand on his head and the other around his neck. Maybe that helped?"

Luca pulled out the egg to check if it was okay.

1:0

"Ha! We've just won two points!" Luca said.

"I am pretty sure it was something I did." Zane nodded sagely. "But enough about that. Anyone notice where my expert navigation skills have taken us?"

Sure enough, they were at the foot of Wisdom Mountain.

Flapping his wings, Zane rose into the air. "Race you to the top, Yaz. Last one there is a rotten Thunder Egg."

"Flying is way easier than climbing the mountain," Zane yelled as he whooshed up to the Dragon Cave at the top of Wisdom Mountain. "I can't see Yazmine, but I bet we beat her by a mile. She can fly, but beast wings can't compete with dragon wings."

A moment later, Zane landed on the rocky platform outside the Dragon Cave's entrance.

"Told you!" he hooted as Luca slipped off his back, carefully clasping the bag with the egg.

"Told you what?" asked Yazmine, lying in the sun and licking a paw as if she'd been there for hours.

"No way!" Zane said. "You must have cheated."

Yazmine stood up and stretched. "Is this how you always react when you lose?"

"I don't know." Zane shrugged. "I've never lost anything before."

"First time for everything," Yazmine said. "Come on, let's go in."

The teammates entered the Dragon Cave. Luca felt a familiar thrill in the pit of his stomach. He would never get used to the fact that they were about to communicate with ancient, wise dragons from long ago. What would they have to say this time?

As Luca's eyes adjusted to the gloom, he saw drawings on the cave walls. Unlike drawings back at home, these ones moved and changed like they were animated. Today they depicted what looked like a party in some sort of huge castle or palace. Dragons, humans, and beasts were dancing and feasting together. Luca could almost hear the sound of the music and smell the delicious things to eat.

"What do you think that is?" Zane asked, pointing a talon at what appeared to be some kind of grand chair.

"It looks like a throne," Luca said. "Maybe

it's where the final Thunder Egg is meant to go?"

"Could be," Yazmine said. "Hey, look at this." With her paw, she tapped a section of the painting, up above the feasting scene. It was blurry and hard to make out. "It looks like a dragon with a human on its back, fighting a . . . What is that? It looks like a human riding a black cloud."

"And check out those things they're holding. Are they sticks? Swords?" Zane wondered, straining his long neck to get a better look.

Luca felt a jolt of excitement. "Maybe it's what the birds were talking about! You know, an upcoming battle. It's GOT to have something to do with the prophecy, right?"

Yazmine leapt into the ring of stones in the center of the cave. “Step inside the circle,” she urged the others. “Let’s see if the Ancient Ones can explain.”

Luca and Zane joined Yazmine inside the ring of stones. Instantly, a noise like a distant storm echoed around them. There were voices swirling in the noise, too. But the words kept slipping away from Luca.

He was disappointed he couldn’t understand what was being said. But he wasn’t surprised. He knew that only dragons can understand the Ancient Ones. It would be up to Zane to translate this time.

Zane had a look of amazement on his face. “I can hear them! I wasn’t sure I believed you guys when you said you understood them. But it's true!"

Yazmine snorted. "Why would we make up something like that?"

"Sssshhh," Zane said, suddenly sounding like a strict teacher. "This is important."

Yazmine looked like she might explode. Luca shot her a warning glance. Yes, Zane was annoying, but the next step of this game depended on what he heard.

Zane frowned. "They're talking about the final Thunder Egg. They say none of the eggs will hatch until this last one is returned to its throne."

"Throne! So that grand chair in the painting *is* a throne. Where is it, exactly?" Luca asked, pulling the Thunder Egg from the bag.

Was the crack even bigger than before?

Gulping, Luca turned the egg over and looked at the map on the other side. "Do they say where we should go?"

"To the walled city of Dracopolis," reported Zane. "It was once the glorious capital of Imperia. A place where humans, beasts, and dragons lived happily side by side. But now the city is nearly deserted. Everyone has been pushed out. Only fear remains."

Luca thought about the empty streets on the other side of that huge stone wall. The buildings too vast for humans to live in. The monstrous Fear Stalker. He shivered. That had to be Dracopolis!

A new icon lit up on the map.

Zane tilted his head as he listened. "They're saying someone will help us, but that we'll have to be careful we find the right person. Someone with mirrors on their eyes—whatever that means." There was a pause, then, "Yikes!"

"What?" Luca asked, not really wanting to hear the answer.

"Dartsmith lives in Dracopolis! At least, *I think* that's what the voices are saying."

Luca and Yazmine exchanged a look. If only they could understand the Ancient Ones themselves. It was frustrating relying on Zane for something so important.

"Anything else?" Yazmine urged. "Make sure you tell us everything."

"I think that's it," Zane said. Then he paused. "Hang on, there is something else. There's some game we have to play against Dartsmith."

Yazmine shook her head. "That can't be right. We're already doing that!"

There was a strange look in Zane's gray dragon eyes. Was it *fear*?

"This is different," he said quietly. "They're saying we must battle Dartsmith in Dracopolis."

"Battle?" Luca repeated.

“What sort of battle?” Yazmine asked.

Zane shrugged apologetically as the roaring wind died down. “Sorry, I didn’t catch that part.”

The three teammates looked at one another as they slowly walked out of the cave.

“Is it just me,” muttered Luca, “or do you two get the feeling this whole game is about to get harder?”

Outside, Yazmine launched into the air. "Let's go! Luca, can you keep an eye on the egg to make sure we're heading the right way?"

Luca settled onto Zane's broad dragon back and pulled out the Thunder Egg. He groaned. It didn't matter how careful he was, the crack just seemed to grow bigger each time he checked.

"No stunts this time," he told Zane as they

rose into the air. "We've got to at least try to get the egg to Dracopolis in one piece!"

The group flew in silence, heading toward the flashing city icon on the egg's surface. They were all deep in their own thoughts. It was clear they had a huge challenge ahead of them, even if they didn't quite know what it was.

Luca gazed down at Imperia below. To the south was the volcano where they'd had their adventure with the Magma Mamba. They'd placed the first Thunder Egg in a fiery nest within the volcano itself. In the opposite direction was snow-covered North Gelida, where they'd battled the Avalanche Wolf. Squinting, Luca could just make out the towering ice sculpture where they'd delivered the second Thunder Egg.

Luca turned to look straight ahead. There, looming larger by the second, were the glittering towers and buildings of Dracopolis. The city was surrounded by its tall stone wall.

The Thunder Egg glowed, as if sensing they were drawing near. Many emotions tumbled inside Luca. It was amazing to be so close to fulfilling the prophecy. He, Zane, and Yaz had always seemed an unlikely team. But they'd achieved so much!

At the same time, Luca was nervous. They had not beaten Dartsmith yet. And Luca knew Dartsmith would do whatever he could to win.

“Look!” Yazmine called, pointing a paw downward. Below them sprawled a giant marketplace, set up outside the city wall. Rows of colorful tents stretched in all directions. Luca could see all sorts of wares laid out for sale. There were stalls selling herbs, spices, and bright bolts of fabric, and others were piled high with teapots and shiny saucepans. One shop was entirely devoted to hats of every style, color, and shape.

A curious mix of smells floated in the air. Perfume, spices, yummy things to eat. Humans and beasts large and small wandered among the stalls while the sellers called out their prices.

“Prepare for landing!” Zane announced as

he whooshed down to the edge of the bazaar. Yaz landed neatly beside him. The clanging noise of the market had been deafening. But now everyone was silent, staring in astonishment at the new arrivals.

Luca felt his face go red. He hated being the center of attention! But as usual, Zane did not mind one bit. He tilted back his silver-gray head and roared triumphantly, filling the air with fire and smoke.

The crowd erupted into cheers, and a chant began, growing louder by the second.

Dra-gon Games!

Dra-gon Games!

A figure pushed through the crowd to the front. It was a girl wearing pants and boots like Luca. Her hair was pulled into a long braid, tied off with an orange scarf. She was wearing strange round goggles with mirrored lenses.

She beamed at the group. “Finally! We’ve been waiting a long time for this moment. You are here to fulfill the prophecy. I can’t wait to see you beat Dartsmith and return the third Thunder Egg.”

“Um, yes,” Luca mumbled. All this was reminding him how much depended on them not messing up.

“I hope you’re good fighters,” the girl continued. “And as you know, you won’t be able to get into the castle with the egg unless you win the Dragon Games first."

Yazmine shot a look at Zane.

"Didn't I tell you that part?" Zane asked. "The Ancient Ones said that if we lose against Dartsmith, we also lose all our points. We need to have at least three points to be able to return the final egg. So if we lose the battle, all our efforts will have been in vain."

"You did forget that small detail," Yazmine growled.

Luca turned to the girl. "Do you know where we're supposed to go? For the Dragon Games battle, I mean?"

The girl laughed. "Not so fast! You have to choose your sword first. I have the best selection in all Imperia. Follow me, I'll take you to my shop."

The crowd parted as Luca, Yazmine, and Zane followed the girl through the crowded bazaar.

"Good luck," people murmured as they passed by.

"Dartsmith has been bad news for Imperia," said one man.

"We hope you beat him once and for all!" a strange-looking beast added.

Luca really, really hoped so, too!

The girl stopped in front of a stall right next to the city wall. It was bigger, and a lot darker, than most of the other stalls.

"Okay," she said cheerily to Luca. "Come

in and select your weapon. The first one you touch is the one you must take. So please choose carefully."

She turned and walked into the shop. Luca and Yaz started to follow but Zane stopped them.

"What is it?" Yaz asked. "Why are you looking like that?"

"Are we sure this isn't Dartsmith?" Zane whispered. "We know he's good at disguises. Those goggles make me suspicious. Maybe this is his best disguise yet!"

Zane had a point. Dartsmith had fooled them before.

"Plus, isn't it kind of weird that we haven't seen him since we've been here this time?"

Zane continued, smoke trailing from his nostrils. "We haven't even seen his drones! This whole setup could be a trap."

Yaz shook her head. "My beast instincts are telling me she's trustworthy."

"Well, my dragon instincts are telling me to be careful," Zane retorted. "I'm going to find out. I'll just make her take off the goggles. We need to see if she has Dartsmith's blue eyes."

Zane pushed his large body into the shop.

"Don't!" Luca said, rushing after Zane. There was a clatter as he knocked into something.

"Hey!" the girl cried as Zane reached out a talon and somehow managed to pull off her goggles.

"Zane, she's not Dartsmith!" Luca said.

Laughing, the girl turned toward them. "I'm definitely not Dartsmith."

Even in the gloom, Luca could see that she had very unusual eyes. They were almond shaped and deep purple. There was a warmth to them that Luca knew Dartsmith could never fake.

"My name's Allie, and believe me, I'm on your side," said the girl. "I'm part of the BBD."

When the others looked at her blankly, she showed them the bright orange scarf tied to her braid. "BBD stands for 'Bring Back Dragons.' The flame-colored scarf is our secret symbol. Our contact in the Outside World told us you were on your way to Dracopolis." Allie looked over Luca's shoulder. "I see you've selected your weapon for the battle."

Allie strode over and picked up what Luca had knocked over before. "Unusual choice. I expected you to go for something more impressive. But I am sure you know what's best to beat Dartsmith."

In the girl's hands was a short, rusty-looking sword with a bent tip. Luca's hopes sank to the bottom of his boots. His "weapon" looked like it was barely up to cutting an apple, let alone going head-to-head with Dartsmith.

From outside came a loud creaking sound. Something heavy was being dragged across the ground. Then a big cheer erupted.

"What's going on?" Yaz asked from the doorway, where she was keeping guard.

"The city gates are opening!" Allie's face flushed with excitement. "It's time for the Dragon Games to begin. Here, you take this."

Allie handed the rusty sword to Luca, who tucked it into his waistband.

Allie strode out of the shop and through the jostling crowd. The others followed. It seemed like everyone was heading in the same direction. People and beasts looked at Luca and his friends as they passed, smiling and nodding encouragement. Every now and then, Luca spotted a flame-colored scarf shoved into a pocket, tied around a neck, or holding back a ponytail. This warmed him inside. They had some supporters, at least!

Up ahead, Luca saw the massive wooden doors to the city. Humans and beasts were streaming through.

"Um, couple of questions," Luca said, hurrying to keep up with Allie. "What exactly does this competition involve?"

Allie shot him a surprised look. "You don't know? It's aerial jousting."

"Jousting?" said Luca. The word rang a bell. "That's where you charge at someone and try to whack them off their horse, right?"

"Pretty much," said Allie, weaving between two giant ratlike beasts who were squeaking with anticipation as they scurried toward the open gate. "Except you'll be doing it in midair on the back of your dragon, of course."

Luca thought back to the image on the walls of the Dragon Cave. The figure riding the dragon must have been him! And that menacing cloudlike shape? That had to be Dartsmith and his drones.

Luca looked at the sword he'd accidentally selected. It looked even shorter than before.

"Let's get one thing clear," Zane said, coming up alongside them. "I am not *his* dragon. We are all equal on this team—although I guess I am a *tiny* bit more important at the moment. I'll be the one returning the Thunder Egg to its nest, after all."

"So what are the rules?" asked Yaz, neatly dodging a young boy selling what looked like popcorn, except the kernels were huge, purple, and kept springing out of the bags.

"Even if there were rules, do you really think

Dartsmith would stick to them?" Allie laughed. "The only rule is to stay in the air. If any part of you touches the ground, you'll instantly be taken to the Nightmare Labyrinth. Heard of it?"

"No," said Luca. "But it doesn't sound like much fun."

"It's really not," Allie agreed.

The group arrived at the gates. A wide street led up into the heart of Dracopolis. It looked different from last time Luca was here. The formerly deserted city was now teeming with beasts and humans, all talking and laughing excitedly as they hurried along. Up ahead, Luca could saw the crowd was gathering. The noise of their voices bounced off the surrounding buildings.

"That's the town square, where the joust will be held," Allie explained, coming to a stop. "We'll need to part ways now. If Dartsmith sees me helping you, I'll be dragged off to the Nightmare Labyrinth myself." Allie waved. Before she disappeared into the crowd, she yelled, "Remember, once you're in the air, do NOT touch the ground!"

Luca had never felt less prepared for anything in his life. "Do you think you're allowed to fight alongside us?" he asked Yazmine as he jumped onto Zane's back. Every inch of him was tingling with nervous excitement. "Three against one doesn't seem fair."

"Like Allie said, there's no way Dartsmith

will play fair," growled Yazmine, lashing her tail as she leapt into the air. "Anyway, there are no rules apart from not touching the ground."

"We've always worked as a team in Imperia," agreed Zane, following Yazmine into the air. "I say we stick together."

The roar of Imperians grew steadily louder as Luca, Zane, and Yaz approached the edge of the town square. Luca felt his pulse quicken. Holding on to Zane's neck with one hand, he pulled his sword from his belt with the other. He sighed at the stumpy, beaten-up weapon. How was he supposed to knock Dartsmith out of the sky with this old thing?

"Don't look so worried, Luca," said Yazmine, flying up alongside.

"Are you saying that because you think I've got a chance against Dartsmith?" Luca asked hopefully.

"No, I'm saying it because the Fear Stalker will be around here somewhere," Yazmine replied. "One whiff of you, and it'll dip you in hot sauce and have you as a snack."

"Thanks," muttered Luca. "Thanks a lot."

Zane soared up high above the square in a showy sweep. The crowd erupted in cheers. Luca looked down, the bag containing the Thunder Egg clutched closely to his thumping heart. There were so many people—and beasts—down there, all with their eyes (sometimes multiple pairs) on him and his teammates. There were patches of bright orange everywhere.

A man stepped into the middle of the square, his arms raised for quiet.

"Beasts and humans, I am the referee of this special event!" he yelled in a booming voice. "The Dragon Games are about to begin."

The crowd stomped their feet and hollered. The referee had to wait until the noise died down before continuing.

He pointed to where Luca and his friends were hovering. "On my left, we have the Outsiders."

There was a pause, then the crowd clapped politely.

"Lots of them want us to win," Zane said softly. "They're just too afraid of Dartsmith to show it."

A hush fell over the crowd and the air felt cooler. A murmur rose on the opposite side of the town square. Then the crowd parted and a thin figure stalked through: a boy with a pointed nose and extremely blue eyes. Dartsmith. Luca heard Yaz draw in a sharp breath. Even Zane seemed to tense up. A black cape billowed as he made his way to the center. He held a huge, shiny sword. It was covered in gleaming buttons and cruel-looking hooks.

"And on my right," the referee bellowed, "is our leader, Dartsmith!"

The crowd cheered much louder this time, but Luca caught glimpses of flame-colored cloth being waved. They definitely had supporters down there.

"To win this battle, you must not only stay off the ground," the referee continued, "you must also win THREE points against your opponent."

A loud buzzing sound filled the air, and the sky grew darker. A mass of drones flew over the crowd. They headed straight to Dartsmith and began rapidly clipping together. Soon, a platform made from drones had formed. Dartsmith stepped calmly onto it and the mega-drone rose up into the air. The sound of its many mechanical wings buzzing was horrible.

Luca couldn't help noticing: Every single drone had a point that was bigger and sharper than Luca's pathetic sword.

“And you thought we’d outnumber Dartsmith,” Yaz muttered. “He’s got at least a hundred drones helping him. All of them armed, too!”

The referee looked left and right. “Are both teams ready?”

“Ready as we’ll ever be,” Luca said, clutching his little sword.

Zane threw back his head and roared, sending the crowd into a frenzy.

"The games will begin on the count of three," announced the man. "One. Two—"

With a yell, Dartsmith lunged forward on his drone platform, swinging his gleaming sword.

"Hey, we didn't even get to three!" protested Zane.

"Rules are for losers." Dartsmith cackled.

Zane swooped as Dartsmith tried to smash the sword over his head. He missed, but the sword caught the tip of his tail. Zane yelped and somersaulted backward. Luca gripped on tightly with one hand, holding the bag and his sword with the other.

"I've got you," called Yaz, flying underneath Zane to stop his somersaulting.

Dartsmith wheeled around and again flew at the trio. Zane lurched to the side just in time, narrowly avoiding another blow from Dartsmith's sword.

"I think my tail is sprained," Zane said in a low voice. "My balance is all wrong."

"Ha! You Outsiders are hopeless!" Dartsmith taunted.

"It's okay," said Yaz, ignoring Dartsmith and sounding as though Zane getting injured was no biggie. "I'll help guide you. And Luca will knock Dartsmith off his platform. Won't you, Luca?"

Luca didn't have time to respond before something sharp and gleaming zipped past.

"What was THAT?" he gasped.

"The drones are shooting darts at us!" Yaz groaned.

Sure enough, Dartsmith's drones were firing their spikes at them. The moment one was released, another instantly grew in its place. The air was soon filled with gleaming metal spears.

Luca raised his sword and swished at them. The spikes exploded as soon as they made contact with the sword's blade.

"Point to the Outsiders!" announced the referee.

The score magically appeared in midair for everyone to see.

0:1

Luca grinned. Maybe this rusty thing wasn't useless after all!

But there was no time for celebrating. Dartsmith was heading right for them.

"Charge!" yelled Zane. Despite his tail, he galloped bravely through the air at Dartsmith. Luca thrust out his sword, determined to push Dartsmith off his mega-drone platform. But just as he was about to make contact, Zane's damaged tail sent him spiraling off course again. Below, everyone gasped and rose to their feet, alarm and excitement rippling through the crowd as Zane and Luca tumbled toward the ground.

"Point to Dartsmith!" the referee boomed.

11

Yaz just managed to fly beneath them before they slammed onto the cobblestones below. She righted Zane, and they headed higher again.

"Come on, you pathetic lumps of metal!" Dartsmith yelled, stomping his foot on his drone platform. "Fire at double speed!"

A fresh batch of darts rained down on Luca and the others.

"We have to protect Zane's wings!" yelled Yaz. "Zane, if you can't fly, this is game over."

Zane nodded, and Luca felt his muscles tense.

Luca slashed at the spikes with his sword

while Yaz swished them away with her tail, growling furiously. Zane joined in, too, roaring out flames that melted the spikes to glistening liquid as he flew unsteadily in circles.

Luca felt a prickling at the back of his neck. Whirling around, Luca saw Dartsmith's eyes glimmering cruelly.

Luca had been so focused on the spikes, he hadn't seen Dartsmith sneak around behind them!

"Quick, Zane!" he urged. "Swerve to the right."

Zane swerved—but to the left!

"Right! I said RIGHT!" Luca cried. "We're going to crash into that building!"

"I'm trying!" huffed Zane, frantically flapping his wings. "My tail is like my rudder. I can't steer very well now that it's injured."

As they hurtled toward a wooden building at the edge of the square, Luca clenched his eyes shut. He knew he could pass through stone. But could he pass through wood? He was about to find out. He felt Zane screech to a halt. When he opened his eyes, they were on the other side of the building!

Luca breathed a sigh of relief as he heard the referee yell, "Point to the Outsiders!"

1:2

"Nicely played!" Yaz called, flying around to join them. "Can't believe you got through a whole building! But watch out, Dartsmith is coming."

No sooner had she spoken than Dartsmith appeared.

"Hello again."

Grinning nastily, he pressed a button on his shining sword. Instantly, flames leapt from it. The crowd gasped. Dartsmith flew at Zane, swishing his flaming sword from side to side.

"Give up!" he screeched. "You don't stand a chance against me!"

"That's what you think!" Yaz snarled. To Zane she muttered, "Hold my tail as you fly. I'll help us stay on course."

Together, the three friends flew back to the other side of the building. Luca clenched his sword tightly. It was time to finish this game. The next time Dartsmith flew at him, he would be ready. This time, he would knock him off that platform!

Luca didn't have long to wait. A second later, Dartsmith charged at them, his sword high in the air. Luca's stomach clenched as Dartsmith pressed a new button. What was the weapon going to do this time?

Flames rushed to the tip of the sword, forming a massive fireball that hurtled toward them. Luca swiped at the fireball with his sword. To his horror, the sword turned to molten metal and dripped away to nothing.

"Point to Dartsmith!"

2:2

The crowd groaned at Luca's setback. More flame-colored scarves had appeared, and many were now being waved defiantly in the air.

Dartsmith was not happy. "You are my subjects!" he yelled furiously at the crowd. "You must be on my side! These Outsiders don't belong here. Anyone who disagrees will be punished."

The crowd fell silent, but there was a restless, angry feeling in the air. Luca was glad to notice that none of the BBD scarves disappeared. He felt a sudden wave of confidence. Dartsmith was a bully and bullies always lose in the end.

The tension left his body. "You're going to lose," Luca said calmly to Dartsmith.

"How dare you!" yelled Dartsmith, turning bright red in the face. He charged at them, the wings of his drone platform beating furiously.

"Zane, duck!" yelled Yazmine. But once again, Zane's damaged tail threw him off course. Instead of dropping out of harm's way, he flew right into Dartsmith's path.

There was a tremendous crash.

Luca gripped on to Zane's steely neck. Something flew past him. Luca gasped. It was Dartsmith, tumbling through the air!

"Catch me, metallic servants!" Dartsmith commanded. He reached out his hands, desperately looking for something to hold on to. But as the drones approached, Zane blasted them with his fiery breath.

Smoldering, twisted metal clattered to the ground. And so did Dartsmith!

"Point to the Outsiders!" announced the referee, sounding gleeful.

2:3

"And Dartsmith is out of bounds!" he giddily continued. "He loses all his points. Soldiers! Take him to the Nightmare Labyrinth."

As Dartsmith lay sprawled on the ground, the crowd leapt to its feet, roaring and screaming with delight. There was no stopping them now.

A group of burly soldiers marched onto the square and grabbed Dartsmith.

“Get your hands off me! I will not go to the Nightmare Labyrinth!” Dartsmith yelled.

But he clearly had no choice. As he was dragged off, he turned to look at Luca and his friends as they landed in the middle of the town square.

“This isn’t over yet!” he yelled.

“Feels pretty over to me!” Zane roared back.

But Luca had noticed something. Panic clutched at him. “The egg!” He held up the empty bag. “It must have fallen out when we crashed into Dartsmith.”

“I can see it,” Yazmine said, her voice grim.

Luca followed her gaze. The egg was lying in the middle of the square.

Hordes of Imperians were surging into the square. The precious egg was about to get stomped on!

Now that Dartsmith had been taken away, the crowd was whooping with delight. Humans and beasts raced into the town square, cheering, dancing, and hugging. Flame-colored scarves fluttered boldly in the air.

"Dartsmith is gone!"

"He's finally been defeated!"

"Zane, quick! We need to rescue the Thunder Egg," Luca said.

But before they could make it there, the egg was scooped up by someone else. Allie.

"Is this what I think it is?" she asked breathlessly as she ran over and carefully handed the egg to Luca.

"Yep. The final Thunder Egg," Yaz confirmed. "But look! The map's not working!"

The etched lines on the back of the egg were flickering, impossible to read. A tendril of steam was curling up from the egg. "How are we going to find the throne room now?"

Allie grinned. "I know where it is. It's in Fear Castle. At least, that's what folks around here call it. It's where Dartsmith lives. I mean, where he *used* to live. It's over there."

They turned to look where she was pointing.

There, set on the highest point of the walled city, was an imposing stone castle. It was gray and full of menace. Tall towers protected it on all sides. It did not look at all welcoming.

"You'll have to take the northern spiral staircase to reach the throne room."

"Thanks, Allie," Luca said. "We appreciate everything you've done for us." Then he turned to his teammates. "Let's go."

He did not add the words ringing in his head. *Before we lose our courage.*

In silence, the trio flew toward the castle. The closer they got, the more hostile it appeared. Just looking at it made Luca's skin prickle.

"Okay," said Zane as they landed out front. "Let's get this done."

"Slight hitch," Yazmine said. "Look who's here."

Thick vines twisted around the castle in all directions. Worse, they were spreading across the remaining stones at an alarming speed.

Luca's heart jumped. The Fear Stalker!

"Why is it growing so fast?" growled Yaz.

"I get the feeling this brute of a plant has been feeding on the locals' fear," Luca said. "Looks like fear was Dartsmith's main weapon. Zane, let's fly through the wall. That'll be quicker than trying to find a window or door that's not covered by the Fear Stalker."

"Fine for you two," Yazmine pointed out. "But what about me?"

Luca grinned. “Fly up close, Yaz. I’ve got an idea. Zane, I know your tail is injured, but can you try to hover in one spot?”

Yaz flew as close as she could without getting her wings caught in Zane’s. Carefully, Luca got onto his knees and then his feet. He was now standing on Zane’s back, midair. Once he had his balance, Luca took a wide step so he had one foot on Yazmine’s back, one on Zane’s.

“Now my superpower will cover all of us,” Luca said.

“Or,” said Yazmine, “you’ll end up doing the splits for the first time. Or we’ll just splatter against the wall.”

"That won't happen," Luca said firmly.

He hoped he sounded more confident than he felt! The Fear Stalker's vines were moving rapidly, covering more of the castle walls by the second.

"Let's do this!" Zane and Yazmine gave their wings a careful flap. Having Yazmine by his side seemed to help Zane fly straight. But it was still very difficult for Luca to keep his balance as they flew along. Luca bent his knees and leaned forward. This just had to work!

As they approached the castle wall, Luca scrunched shut his eyes.

"Let's do this!" he yelled. There was a slight feeling of pressure—like pushing through water—and when he opened his eyes again, they were inside the castle. He hadn't even fallen off!

"I'll be honest," purred Yazmine, still hovering in midair next to Zane. "I one hundred percent did not think that would work."

"I one hundred percent knew it would," said Zane, puffing two impressive smoke rings. "The sillier Luca's ideas sound, the more likely they are to succeed."

"Thanks, Zane," said Luca, jumping off their backs and landing on the stone floor of the castle. "I think."

It was dark inside the castle, but Luca could make out movement on the castle walls. The Fear Stalker's vines were winding through cracks and slit windows. New shoots grew rapidly into thick tendrils, whipping back and forth in the air as if feeling for where Luca and his teammates were.

"Which way do we go?" Zane asked. "I can't see a thing!"

"I can see," Yazmine said. "Must be my beast eyes. That way is north, so according to Allie we should take that staircase. Looks like it takes us up one of the castle towers."

Together, the group ran up the wide spiral staircase, with the grasping vines of the Fear Stalker right behind them.

Don't be afraid, Luca kept trying to tell himself. But it was easier said than done! He could sense that his teammates were struggling, too.

Around and around the trio went up the stairs until, finally, the twirling staircase ended, and Luca, Yazmine, and Zane found themselves in a perfectly circular room.

As they leapt inside, Yaz slammed her weight against the door to close it behind them. Severed vines fell to the floor, writhing.

Luca looked around.

On the curved walls were intricate drawings of three very different dragons. They were seated side by side and each wore a golden crown.

In the center of the room was an ornately carved chair. It was very old and dusty, but there was no disguising its grandeur.

"We've definitely found the throne room.

And the throne!" Yazmine said, her voice hushed with awe. "This is it. We've almost completed the quest!"

Luca held out the cracked Thunder Egg to Zane.

"You're the dragon this time, Zane," he said. "Like the Ancient Ones say: It takes a dragon to make a dragon. It's your turn."

Luca thought he'd be envious of Zane. After all, Zane would get to return the final egg and fulfill the prophecy.

But now that it was about to happen, all Luca felt was pride. They'd all achieved this. It didn't matter who actually put the final egg on the throne.

Zane turned toward Luca's outstretched

hands and took the egg in his mouth.

"Don't eat it by mistake," Luca joked, expecting Zane to roll his eyes at him.

But Zane's eyes were focused on something behind Luca.

Luca spun around just as there was a loud bang. The Fear Stalker had smashed down the door and was spilling into the room.

A terrible doubt clutched at Luca. *What if we fail at the last moment? What if all our hard work comes to nothing?*

Thick vines tumbled into the room, feeling their way along the floor like leafy hands. With a snarl, Yazmine jumped at the vines, biting and tearing at them.

"Zane and Luca, just get that Thunder Egg

in place!" she growled through a mouthful of leaves.

The boys did not need telling twice. Luca jumped on Zane's back, and, with a flap of his wings, Zane half flew, half leapt over to the golden throne. He landed lightly in front of it. Looking at the seat, Luca saw a pattern on the ancient fabric. It was a nest.

Instantly, all Luca's fears fell away.

"We've done it. We've actually done it," whooped Zane. "I had my doubts for a moment there. But I should've known we'd win in the end."

Behind them Yazmine yelped in surprise. Looking around, Luca saw the Fear Stalker's branches shriveling away to nothing. The leaves curled and fell to the ground.

"Yaz, come over here," Luca called. "The whole team should be together for this!"

Yaz dropped the wilted vines in her mouth and leapt over to the throne. Zane, being careful for once in his life, placed the egg on the throne in the middle of the ancient nest design. For a moment, everyone and everything in the throne room seemed to hold its breath. There was an almighty crack. Luca was thrown to the ground as the castle trembled and shook. A white-hot blast lit up the room for an instant. Then the throne room was plunged into total darkness.

Blinking, Luca staggered to his feet. Was he back at school? No, he was still in the throne room. That was strange. The room was dark, but he could see something glowing.

The Thunder Egg had split into two perfect halves. The insides glittered with rings of colorful crystals. The outer ring was clear, growing to a deep purple near the middle. The very center was hollow. Hollow, but not empty.

There, nestled in the heart of the Thunder Egg was a tiny dragon.

"Wow." Yazmine sighed, padding up on Luca's left.

"Look at the little guy!" Zane crooned, leaning over Luca's other shoulder. "He's so cute!"

There was a loud ripping sound from behind them. The team of three turned around in time to see a zigzag flash of light. Luca watched in amazement as the air seemed to crack open. A huge dragon stepped through the crack. It was even bigger than Zane and was a dramatic jade green.

"Actually, this baby is a 'she,'" said the dragon.

Yazmine gasped. "Wait, I know that voice! Ms. Long! Is that you?"

"Correct, Yazmine," replied the bright green dragon.

"You're a *dragon*?" Zane spluttered.

The dragon laughed, sending a stream of green smoke into the air. "I'm surprised you didn't figure it out earlier," she said. "As you know, when Dartsmith took control of Imperia he banished the dragons. We were forced to live as humans in your world. But everything has changed now that you have fulfilled the prophecy."

Luca exhaled, trying to let that sink in.

Ms. Long continued, "Now that the three dragon rulers have hatched, they will be in charge of the three regions of Imperia. This dragon will rule over Dracopolis." Ms. Long looked over at the tiny dragon, a proud expression on her jade-colored face. "The second will protect North Gelida. The third will guard Vesva, the volcano area you visited on your first adventure."

Ms. Long turned to look out the throne room's window. "Come, you can see the banished dragons returning to Imperia."

Luca, Yazmine, and Zane hurried over to the narrow window. The once-deserted city was now brimming with life. It was a breathtaking sight. With a sound like ripping fabric, large gashes appeared all across the sky. Through each rip emerged a dragon.

Down below, a party was underway. Imperians were descending on the bazaar, bringing food and drink. Delicious smells wafted through the air. Musicians were playing happy, triumphant music.

Luca spotted Allie, doing a wild dance with an enormous beast. Then he laughed. It was the leaf-bear he'd chatted with in their last adventure. But this time the creature's leaves were broad and green.

The whole scene reminded Luca of something.

"It's like the painting in the Dragon Cave," said Yaz, seeming to read his mind. "I thought it was depicting the past. But maybe it was showing us the future?"

"It was both," said Ms. Long. "Imperia used to be a happy place. Dartsmith changed that when he took control."

A question had been nagging at Luca for a while. "Why did Dartsmith hate dragons so much?" he asked.

Ms. Long paused for a moment. "It's a long and complicated story," she said eventually. "I'll tell you one day. But now it's time to return home."

"I guess you'll stay to look after the baby dragon?" Zane asked.

The little creature was peering above the broken shell curiously. Ms. Long laughed, flames curling from her mouth and bathing the room in a warm glow.

"Don't be fooled by her size," Ms. Long warned. "This dragon, along with her two brothers, is more powerful than any creature in Imperia. And now there are plenty of dragons to keep her company."

As she spoke, colored puffs of smoke exploded in the room and two new dragons appeared. The throne room was getting cramped!

One of the dragons held a silver bowl in its jaws. Steam rose from the vessel, filling the air with a delicate perfume. The dragon padded carefully over to the throne and placed the bowl before the tiny dragon, who breathed in the curling steam.

Ms. Long turned to Zane. "So, in answer to your question, no. You haven't gotten rid of me yet. I will be returning to your world. I will even continue to be your teacher. The school is an important portal between your world and Imperia. It is my duty to protect it."

Zane shrugged his dragon shoulders. "You're kind of my favorite teacher." He glared at Luca and Yazmine. "But if you guys breathe a word of that, you're in big trouble."

Yazmine ignored him. "How do we get back?" she asked. "Usually it happens when we put the Thunder Egg in its nest."

"This time is different," replied their dragon teacher, stretching out her magnificent jade wings. They almost touched the walls of the room. “Stand below my wings. We’ll travel together.”

Luca took one last look at the celebrations below. He got the feeling festivities were going to last all night. It was pretty amazing to think that it was all because of their team effort!

“Come on, Luca,” Yazmine called.

Luca hurried over to where the others were standing under the vast span of Ms. Long’s shining wings. Another question burst from him.

“Ms. Long, will we come back to Imperia?”

He was so proud they’d fulfilled the prophecy. But he’d be sad to leave Imperia for good.

“I cannot answer that for sure,” their

teacher replied. "But there are still battles to be fought here."

Then, with a multicolored flash of light, the floor dropped away, and Luca began to fall . . .

Once again, Luca found himself on the ground, blinking. He was in the school cafeteria. Yaz and Zane were back in their human forms, looking as bewildered as Luca felt.

Ms. Long stood before them, her arms crossed. "You three are still here?" But there was a smile on her face. "The bell is about to ring. Make sure you're in class on time."

She turned and strode away, her shiny green shoes clacking loudly.

Luca, Yazmine, and Zane looked at one

another. Whenever they returned from Imperia, Luca found it hard to believe all that had actually happened.

But it did! he told himself. *We fulfilled the prophecy and brought peace to Imperia.* It wasn't bad work for one lunchtime.

"Well, we'd better get going, I guess," Yaz said, sounding reluctant. "We don't want to be late. We all know what a dragon Ms. Long can be, right?"

"We sure do." Luca grinned.

Zane held up a hand. "Hang on. Have you forgotten something?"

Luca and Yazmine looked at him blankly.

"Our chant!" said Zane. "Come on, guys. Say it with me:

Who's the best, to say the least?

Team Dragon, Human, Beast!"

Yazmine laughed and shook her head. "That chant is not getting any better."

"Are you kidding?" Zane said. "It's great. And so are we! I'd team up with you guys again any day."

"Me too," said Yazmine.

Luca just nodded. He didn't quite trust himself to speak. There was a chance they would never return to Imperia. But deep in his heart, Luca had a strong feeling they would.

Another clawsome series by the author of Dragon Games!

Turn the page for a special sneak peek!

Azmina lay on her stomach in her brand-new backyard. The weather was warm for fall, but Azmina didn't feel the sun on her skin. She didn't notice a dog barking nearby. She didn't even hear her mom singing as she unpacked boxes in the house they had just moved into.

A strange sound had caught Azmina's

attention. The sound blocked out everything else. It was as if someone was whispering the first line of a song.

Magic Forest, Magic Forest, come explore . . .

Through a gap in the back fence, Azmina could see the edge of a forest. Was the music coming from there?

Azmina wasn't used to lying around on the grass, admiring trees. She thought of herself as a city girl, through and through. Well, she used to, anyway. She wasn't quite sure who she was in this new place yet. Back in the city she was always on the go: Singing lessons, playing soccer with her friends, organizing sleepovers.

But now, there wasn't anyone to organize sleepovers with. Everything had changed when she and her mom moved. Azmina liked the kids at her new school, but she didn't have any besties yet.

In school, she had been assigned to a table with two other girls named Willa and Naomi. Somehow Azmina just knew that she was meant to be friends with them. She could feel it, fizzing like bubbles in a soft drink, deep in her stomach. But she wasn't quite sure how to make it happen.

Azmina sighed. She knew that friendships took time, but she hated being the new girl.

Magic Forest, Magic Forest, come explore . . .

Azmina sat up. The singing was clearer now. It was definitely coming from the forest! But it was different from any music Azmina had heard before. The melody was like the songs of a thousand birds and the babble of a river all mixed together with the rustling of leaves.

Azmina jumped up and ran to the back fence. She leaned over to get a closer look.

Because she was from the city, she'd never seen a real forest up close before. She couldn't take her eyes off it! The leaves had turned the colors of fall. These were Azmina's favorites—brilliant red, fiery orange, and best of all, bright yellow. The forest floor looked like it was covered with treasure.

There was one tree that caught Azmina's attention. It was the tallest of all, with long and graceful branches. The tree's leaves shone as if they were made of pure gold. Azmina felt a little shiver of excitement run up her back. There was something special about that tree. Something magical.

As she gazed into the forest, Azmina realized there were other curious things about it.

"I can smell flowers," Azmina muttered to herself. "But that doesn't make sense! Most of the flowers are gone now that it's fall."

But that wasn't even the strangest thing. Azmina thought she could smell pineapples and mangoes. Azmina didn't know much about forests, but she was pretty sure pineapples and mangoes didn't grow around here!

Now that she was closer, Azmina could hear more singing coming from the forest.

Magic Forest, Magic Forest, come explore.
Magic Forest, Magic Forest, hear my roar!

Hear my roar? What could that mean?

Azmina repeated the words out loud, softly

at first: “Magic Forest, Magic Forest.” But each time she said them, her voice got louder. One of the golden leaves on the tallest tree spun up

into the air. It danced through the sky, swishing this way and that, leaving a glowing trail behind it.

Azmina watched as the leaf looped its way closer. When the leaf was above her, she leapt up and grabbed it. It was warm from the sunlight. Azmina's fingertips tingled.

Suddenly, she knew just what to do. Her voice rang out strong and true as she began to sing:

Magic Forest, Magic Forest, come explore.

Magic Forest, Magic Forest, hear my roar!

Instantly, a hot gust of wind swirled around her. Azmina closed her eyes as she was whooshed up into the air, spun around, and then dropped down onto the ground again. It took only a few seconds, but Azmina knew something amazing had happened. Something life-changing.

ABOUT THE AUTHORS

Maddy Mara is the pen name of Australian creative duo Hilary Rogers and Meredith Badger. Hilary is a writer and former publisher; Meredith is a writer, and teaches English as a second language. Together they have written or created many bestselling series for kids. Their most recent series is The Dragon Girls, which has over 1.5 million copies in print, and is available in multiple countries and languages. They both currently live in Melbourne, Australia. Their website is maddymara.com.

DRAGON
GIRLS

THE GLITTER DRAGONS
DRAGON GIRLS
Azmina the Gold
Glitter Dragon
Maddy Mara
SCHOLASTIC

THE GLITTER DRAGONS
DRAGON GIRLS
Willa the Silver
Glitter Dragon
Maddy Mara
SCHOLASTIC

THE GLITTER DRAGONS
DRAGON GIRLS
Naomi the Rainbow
Glitter Dragon
Maddy Mara
SCHOLASTIC

THE TREASURE DRAGONS
DRAGON GIRLS
Mei the Ruby
Treasure Dragon
Maddy Mara
SCHOLASTIC

THE TREASURE DRAGONS
DRAGON GIRLS
Aisha the Sapphire
Treasure Dragon
Maddy Mara
SCHOLASTIC

THE TREASURE DRAGONS
DRAGON GIRLS
Quinn the Jade
Treasure Dragon
Maddy Mara
SCHOLASTIC

THE NIGHT DRAGONS
DRAGON GIRLS
Rosie the
Twilight Dragon
Maddy Mara
SCHOLASTIC

THE NIGHT DRAGONS
DRAGON GIRLS
Phoebe the
Moonlight Dragon
Maddy Mara
SCHOLASTIC

THE NIGHT DRAGONS
DRAGON GIRLS
Stella the
Starlight Dragon
Maddy Mara
SCHOLASTIC

Collect them all!